Must Fly!

When a high-diving dare goes wrong, it signals the start of another myth adventure for Perce, Eddie, Well'ard and – er – Icarus?

Yes, ancient Greece's favourite fly-boy has arrived in the twenty-first century to find Well'ard and Eddie playing ducks and drakes with his very survival. Meanwhile, Andy is working as a test pilot for the looniest inventor in history and it looks as if he's about to come down to earth with a bump (and a few "aargghhhs" and a large splat!).

When Perce tries to get everyone back where they belong, the feathers really start to fly. Can she change history? Will her plan take off? Or will it crash and burn?

A madcap retelling of the Icarus myth from the 2 Steves.

Other books by Steve Barlow & Steve Skidmore

STONE ME! – Barn Owl Books
MIND THE DOOR! – Barn Owl Books
A TOUCH OF WIND! – Barn Owl Books
DON'T LOOK BACK! - Barn Owl Books

TALES OF THE DARK FOREST – HarperCollins
Goodknyght!
Whizzard!
Trollogy!
Knyghtmare!

LOST DIARIES – Harper Collins
The Lost Diary of Henry VIII's Executioner
The Lost Diary of Erik Bloodaxe, Viking Warrior
The Lost Diary of Shakespeare's Ghostwriter

VERNON BRIGHT – Puffin
Vernon Bright and the Magnetic Banana
Vernon Bright and Frankenstein's Hamster
Vernon Bright and the Faster-Than-Light Show
Vernon Bright and the End of the World

STAR BORES – HarperCollins

THE DOOMSDAY VIRUS – Barrington Stoke

FUNNY BUSINESS – Barrington Stoke

Steve Barlow & Steve Skidmore

MUST FLY!

Illustrated by Tony Ross

BARN OWL BOOKS

First published by Barn Owl Books 2007
First published by Puffin Books 1998
ISBN 9781903015650
ISBN 1903015650

Distributed by Frances Lincoln,
4 Torriano Mews, Torriano Avenue, London NW52RZ

Designed by Douglas Martin
Printed and bound in UK by Cox & Wyman

Contents

Chapter One
DO DROP IN · Page 7

Chapter Two
FLYING VISIT · Page 17

Chapter Three
DEAD LOSS · Page 24

Chapter Four
PILOT ERROR · Page 31

Chapter Five
FLIGHT PLAN · Page 37

Chapter Six
A TOUCH OF FLEW · Page 45

Chapter Seven
FEATHERED FRIENDS · Page 52

ChapterEight
BIRD BRAINS · Page 60

Chapter Nine
FLIGHTS OF FANCY · Page 67

Chapter Ten
FLY AWAY HOME · Page 73

Chapter Eleven
SPLASHDOWN · Page 78

Chapter Twelve
FLOATING ON AIR · Page 86

Chapter One

DO DROP IN

"Chicken! Chicken!" Perce's cry rang out across the swimming pool. "Andy's a chicken!"

Andy stared at her. There were times when he really hated Perce. This was definitely one of them. He was feeling fed up anyway – the water in the pool had dissolved all the gel out of his hair and scraggy brown strands of it kept flopping in his eyes. And just to make things worse, Perce was having a go at him.

"Look," he said, "I don't see why I'm a chicken just because I won't go to the top of the high diving board and jump off."

"Cluck, cluck, cluck . . ." Perce rolled onto her back and kicked out, splashing water over Andy.

"Mr Latimer says no one is allowed to go up there."

"Since when did you start taking any notice of teachers? Anyway, it'll liven up the lesson."

Andy had to agree; it had been a boring swimming session. The class had been churning out lengths of the local swimming pool dressed in pyjamas. This was called 'life-saving'. Perce had pointed out to Mr Latimer that if she ever did have to rescue someone from drowning, it was highly unlikely that she'd be wearing pyjamas at the time! Mr Latimer had said that wasn't the point and to stop being so stupid.

"And another thing, sir – what am I going to wear in bed tonight?" Perce had complained. "My pyjamas are soaking wet and stink of chlorine!" Mr Latimer stared at Perce and walked off muttering.

But now it was free time and the rest of the class

happily swam, divebombed each other and generally splashed about. In the deep end, Perce and Andy trod water and bickered.

"If you're so bothered about livening the lesson up, why don't you do it?"

Perce looked Andy straight in the eye. "Because I'm a girl!"

"What sort of an answer is that?"

Perce put on her superior look. "Girls don't have to show off – we know we're better than boys. Boys *have* to show off to try and make themselves look like real men. It's what boys do."

Andy was puzzled. He was sure that Perce's argument had a very large hole in it, but he couldn't quite work out what it was.

"For instance, take Well'ard," continued Perce. "Look what he got for showing off. Banned from swimming for a month." She pointed to Well'ard Wally, the school hard nut, who was sitting fully clothed on a bench at the side of the pool. Well'ard was always in trouble with teachers for "being rude" or "being cheeky" (he claimed to have had one detention slip on which, under Reason for Detention, Mr Latimer had written, "being alive"). Right now he was throwing plastic bricks into the water so that other kids in the class could dive down and "rescue" them. Although more often than not, he threw the bricks *at* the other kids.

"What did he do?" asked Andy

"Oh come on!" exclaimed Perce, "You know what happened last week.

"I was away last week."

"He had a pee in the pool!"

Andy looked incredulously at Perce. "That's not fair to ban him! Everyone knows kids pee in swimming pools.

"Yeah, but not from the high diving board!"

Andy looked in amazement from Well'ard up to the top diving board and back again.

"So that's why we're banned from going up there?"

"Correct."

"What are you two arguing about?" piped up a shrill voice. Andy sculled round and saw Eddie Johnson doggy paddling towards them. Cheerful and accident-prone, Eddie went through life like a small, snub-nosed punch-ball. No matter how hard he was knocked down, he always bounced back.

"I've dared Andy to jump off the high diving board and he won't," Perce told him.

Eddie guffawed. "You chicken!"

Andy smiled like a crocodile. "All right Eddie, what about you doing a dare?"

There was a moment's silence as Eddie realised that he had just put his big foot firmly in his mouth. "Er . . . well . . . er . . ." he stammered.

"Aren't you a real man?" Andy asked pointedly.

Eddie was stung into defence. "Of course I am! What do you want me to do?"

Perce burst into laughter. Not only had she hooked Andy, she'd also caught Eddie on the same hook. Boys are so stupid, she thought to herself.

Andy thought for a moment before his eyes lit up and an evil grin spread slowly across his face. "Do a double somersault off the springboard."

Eddie flinched in horror. He was useless at gymnastics. This dare was worse than jumping off the high diving board.

"It's easy," Andy told him. "All you've got to do is run along the board, bounce on the end, shout 'Geronimo!' and . . ."

"Why 'Geronimo'?"

"How do I know? It's just what you shout when you jump off something."

"Well, I'm not going to jump off anything and you can't make me."

"Cluck, cluck . . ." began Perce.

"All right! I'll do it!"

Eddie swam to the side of the pool and hauled himself out. Checking that Mr Latimer's attention was elsewhere, he stepped gingerly onto the board. From the pool, Andy and Perce catcalled and beckoned him on.

"And now," announced Perce, "live from Ocean World Florida – he leaps like a dolphin! He swims like a seal! He'll do anything for a bucket of fish – let's hear it for the incredible performing Eddie Johnson!"

"Here goes!" Eddie raced along the springboard and bounced into the air. For a moment he hung poised at the height of his leap. Then gravity took hold and he came down, hit the end of the board hard and shot upwards, totally out of control.

"Geronim – OH NOOOOOOOO!"

Eddie's body was spun and twisted by the violence of his leap. He performed several twists, pikes and back somersaults that would have won him an Olympic gold medal . . . if only he hadn't hit the water belly first.

An almighty crack echoed round the pool. Well'ard howled with glee. "Bellyflop! That has *got* to hurt!"

Eddie gave a ghastly sigh as the impact sucked air out of his body quicker than a super turbo vacuum cleaner, and sank beneath the waves.

"Not exactly Flipper, is he?" sniggered Perce.

"Nope," said Andy. "He's more of a Flopper."

Eddie shot to the surface of the pool, trying desperately to gulp down lungfuls of air. Everyone burst out laughing. Perce and Andy watched in hysterics as Eddie floated to the edge of the pool and dragged himself out onto the side where he gave a lifelike impression of a recently caught fish flapping about on a river bank.

Mr Latimer strode over to Eddie.

"What do you think you're doing?"

"Uh, uh, uh," rasped Eddie.

"What?"

"Uh, uh, uh!"

The skin on Eddie's belly was going from pink

to purple. Mr Latimer frowned. "That's a nasty bruise you've got on your stomach."

"It's not his stomach he's worried about, sir," chortled Well'ard, "it's his . . ."

"Thank you, Walter, that will do." Mr Latimer took pity on Eddie. "Come on, let's get you sorted out."

"Yuhs please suh, uh, uh."

Mr Latimer helped the still flapping Eddie towards the changing rooms.

Perce checked that the pool attendant was nowhere in sight. She turned to Andy: "Right. He's done his dare – now it's your turn." She pointed at the high diving board. "Up you go"

Andy peered over the edge of the board and felt dizzy. Why had he let Perce talk him into this? He was frightened of heights. He even felt sick going up an escalator.

Andy shook his head. If he had any sense, he would just step back, climb down to the safety of the ground and tell Perce that he didn't need to prove himself to her or anybody.

"Come on, you chicken!" Perce yelled from below.

Andy felt himself going hot and cold as he was hit by a nasty attack of the machos. "Right, I'll show her!" he hissed.

Taking a deep breath, he ran at the board, leapt into space and hurtled out and downwards.

"Yeehah!" screamed Perce.

"Go Andy!" cheered Well'ard.

Andy heard nothing but the air whizzing by. His legs thrashed wildly as he tried to gain a foothold that wasn't there.

"WHAAAAAHHHHHHHHHH!"

SPLASH!

The centre of the pool seemed to explode upwards and outwards. For a few seconds, Perce was blinded as waves crashed round her head. Spluttering, she blinked the water from her eyes, and looked for Andy. There was no sign of him.

Perce began to feel worried. Perhaps Andy had come down awkwardly and been knocked out. Maybe she'd have to rescue him. But how could she? She wasn't even wearing her pyjamas!

Telling herself not to be so stupid, Perce tried to swim towards Andy's point of entry. She found herself pushing through something that looked like snow floating on the water. She sneezed. Feathers! The surface of the pool was covered with them.

As she tried to work out what was happening a head surged out of the depths of the pool. The spluttering figure turned to face Perce.

"Andy, what's all these . . .?" She recoiled in horror. The question stuck in her throat.

It wasn't Andy. It was someone else!

Chapter Two

FLYING VISIT

People were queuing up to have a go at Perce.

First there was Mr Latimer, who had stormed out of the changing rooms to find out what all the commotion was about. "What's going on here?"

"It was Perce sir!" Well'ard grassed. "She dared Andy to dive off the top board."

Mr Latimer went ballistic. He ranted on for ages about Irresponsible Behaviour and Ruining The

Good Name Of The School ("What good name?" wondered Perce) and made it clear that Perce would be collecting her old age pension before he took her swimming again.

Then there was the attendant, who had bow legs, piggy eyes and a razor hair cut. He went a funny colour when he saw the mess in the pool. "Vandals!" he screamed. "Yobs! Troublemakers! Lowlife! Barbarians!" He tried to tear his hair out, but he couldn't get hold of it.

Next in to bat were the leisure centre manager, the man who cleaned out the pool filters (now clogged with feathers), the whole of the next class who were going to have to wait for their swim while the pool was being cleared, and a lady who'd lost her money in a hot drinks machine and complained to Perce about it because everybody else was yelling at Perce so why shouldn't she?

Nobody seemed at all put out by the fact that the kid in the pool wasn't Andy.

It eventually dawned on Perce that this was because no-one had noticed – except for Well'ard, who had dragged the strange kid out of the pool and hustled him into the changing rooms, gallantly leaving Perce to face the music.

When everyone had finished shouting at her, Perce was allowed to get changed. By the time she had struggled into her clothes and burst through the door into the foyer, Mr Latimer was already checking that no-one was missing. He was moving down the line, wagging his finger to count the class. Eddie (still rubbing his stomach) winked and gave Perce a "thumbs up" sign. He jerked his head sideways at the strange kid standing between himself and Well'ard.

Perce stared in disbelief. The new arrival was at least twenty centimetres taller than Andy, and broader too. She didn't know how Eddie and Well'ard had got him into Andy's clothes, but they must have used some kind of a rammer. Level Five for effort, thought Perce, but Working Towards Level One for good thinking.

Mr Latimer reached the new kid. He stopped counting. He looked bewildered. Eventually, he cleared his throat and said, "Are you . . . er . . . all right . . . er . . . Andrew?"

"He's fine, sir," piped up Well'ard.

"I wasn't asking you, Walter."

"He can't answer you, sir." Well'ard was giving his well known Oscar-winning performance of innocence. "He's got Laughing Jitus."

Mr Latimer was used to Well'ard. "Laryngitis."

"Yes, sir, he's got that an' all. Can't talk, sir."

Mr Latimer seemed about to argue; but when he looked at the strange kid again, his eyes glazed over; he shook his head, and went on down the line.

Perce was dying to talk to Eddie and Well'ard, and to the strange kid (assuming he *did* talk), but on the way back to school she was forced to walk next to Mr Latimer. As soon as she got back to school, Perce was Sent For by the Head. A painful interview followed, during which the Head let it be known that she was Very Disappointed in Perce. Letters Home were mentioned. The Head also made it absolutely clear that if she had her way, Perce would suffer the death of a thousand cuts, and be boiled in oil and burned at the stake, though in what order wasn't clear. Finally coming down from orbit, the Head pronounced sentence (loss of breaks and lunchtimes for three weeks), and told Perce that if she (the Head) heard about any more of this sort of behaviour, then she (Perce) would be Very Sorry.

At lunchtime, Perce was sitting glumly in the punishment room when there was a "*pssst*" noise from the direction of the window and Well'ard poked his nose over the sill.

"I heard you was in the cooler," he hissed. "How long did they give you?"

Perce glanced towards the front of the room. Miss Mills was absorbed in writing reports. Probably trying to remember how many 'l's there are in 'appalling', thought Perce sourly.

From the corner of her mouth, Perce growled, "Three weeks."

"Oh well, could be worse."

"How?"

Well'ard considered for a moment. "Could have been four weeks."

"Push off, Well'ard."

Well'ard hitched himself higher. "You know that kid we pulled out of the pool? He wants to talk to you."

"*I* want to talk to *him*," snarled Perce. "Who is he?"

"Dunno really. He says his name's Icarus."

"OH, NO!"

Perce's anguished howl sent Well'ard tumbling backwards into the bushes and earned her an extra detention for making Miss Mills jab her pen clean through the report form.

"So," said Perce, folding her arms grimly, "who's going to tell me what's going on?"

At the end of the school day, she had grabbed Eddie and Well'ard. With Icarus in tow, they had made for the park to find somewhere quiet for a council of war. Now, Perce stood facing a park bench on which the boys were sitting like the Three Wise Monkeys.

Eddie cleared his throat nervously. "You're not going to like it."

"Try me."

Eddie shrugged and nodded towards Icarus, who looked bewildered and apologetic. "He was on a test flight."

"Go on."

"He told us at lunchtime while you were in detention. He was trying out some new wings for his dad . . ."

"Dead Loss," interrupted Well'ard.

Eddie gave him a pitying look. "Dedalus," he corrected. "Only they didn't work. His dad made him jump off a cliff, and he was falling into the sea, *flap flap flap kersplash*, and then he found himself here."

"It figures." The only good thing about spending her breaks in Solitary was that it had given Perce time to think; she had a few ideas of her own about what had happened at the swimming pool.

Icarus spoke up for the first time. "I think maybe . . ." He stopped. He had a soft, slow voice with a strange musical accent. Perce found herself wanting to hear it again.

"Go on," she said again, not quite so grimly this time.

Icarus looked up at her. "I think maybe, we changed places. I mean, I came to where your friend was, and he went to where I was."

"Yeah?" Well'ard grunted. "Where's that then?"

"At a guess," said Perce, "Ancient Greece. About three thousand years ago . . ."

Chapter Three

DEAD LOSS

As Andy plunged through the surface of the swimming pool, a jet of water shot up his nose nearly causing his brain to explode. Survival instincts took over from his waterlogged mind and he kicked his legs to push himself up towards the surface.

His head broke the water.

"See, Perce, I'm not a chicken!" he yelled out. "I did it! I did . . ."

He stopped and looked around in wide-eyed

astonishment. There was something very, very wrong.

This wasn't the local swimming pool anymore, not unless:

a) someone had quickly taken the roof off to let a hot sun beat down on the water;

b) a fishing fleet had lost its way and turned up in the shallow end;

c) a rocky shoreline had been painted on the pool wall, and

d) it had suddenly got bigger – a lot bigger. Like a few hundred square miles bigger.

Andy shook his head. "I must be dreaming," he thought. "If I shut my eyes and open them again, I'll be back at the swimming pool."

So he did. But he wasn't. When he opened his eyes again, Andy was swimming in a clear blue sea, off a rocky coastline with a scorching sun beating down on him.

He began to get very worried.

"What do you think you're playing at, you stupid boy?"

"Mr Latimer?" Andy span round in the water.

A man in a boat was heading towards him. He

was dressed in a short white tunic. He had a shock of white hair. It certainly wasn't Mr Latimer. It wasn't anyone Andy knew.

"I said, what do you think you're playing at?" The boat drifted close to Andy. The man shook his fists at him. Andy added being frightened to being worried.

"Well? Are you going to splash around enjoying yourself all day? Or are you going to get in the boat?"

It was a strange looking boat. The planks were rough and uneven. The man stood at the back, rowing with a single oar. As Andy struggled on board, he realised he didn't have his swimming trunks on anymore – he was dressed in some sort of white loin cloth.

His mind said this couldn't be happening. Unfortunately, it was being overruled by his eyes, his ears and all the rest of him.

"Where are the wings?" boomed the man. Andy gawped at him. "Answer me, you young idiot!"

"Wings?" spluttered Andy, wondering what he was talking about. "Erm, er . . . on the birds?" he answered hopefully.

"On the birds! On the birds! What are you gab-bling about in Zeus' name? I took the feathers off the birds and put them on the wings."

Andy was losing track of the conversation. "And then you put the wings back on the birds?" he said lamely.

"NO!" yelled the man, "I put the wings on you! I, Dedalus, the greatest inventor of all time, made you a pair of wings, so you could leap off the cliff and fly in the air."

"Dedalus?" Andy flinched. The name definitely rang a bell, but only a very small one. Dedalus was pointing to something over Andy's shoulder. He turned. Andy looked up at the height of the cliff and gawped. "I jumped off there?" he trembled.

"Of course you did." Dedalus looked closely at Andy. "Don't you remember?"

Andy was pretty sure that he'd jumped off a high diving board, but he wasn't going to argue. Maybe he'd wake up soon and get out of this nightmare. He hoped so, but in the meantime, he thought he'd better humour the man who called himself 'Dedalus'.

"Oh yes, of course. I must have banged my head

when I hit the water. It's made everything go fuzzy."

Dedalus harrumphed and looked down at the water. "I suppose the wings have sunk. You couldn't even hold onto them. What sort of son are you?"

"I'm your son?" Andy was gobsmacked.

Dedalus stared at him. "Perhaps the force of the landing has scrambled your wits." He peered into Andy's eyes. "How many fingers am I holding up?"

Andy could see two, but decided to play up his 'injury'.

"Twenty seven!"

"Are you sure?"

"Ah, no sorry . . . there's only thirteen and a half! I thought I was seeing double for a minute."

"Hmm." Dedalus looked suspiciously at Andy. "We'd better get back. We need to return to the workshop and get the spare wings ready. We don't have much time."

As Dedalus rowed back towards the shore, hundreds of thoughts flashed through Andy's head, but the one that kept coming back time and again was a growing suspicion that he was in the middle of another terrible mythological nightmare.

The boat pulled in to a small harbour. Two rough-looking men looked up from the nets they were mending and sniggered.

"Well, look at that," shouted one. "Dedalus has caught a flying fish."

"You're wasting your time, you old crackpot!" yelled the other. "If the gods had meant us to fly, they'd have given us beaks!"

"Wings," corrected the other.

"Right! Wings!"

They fell about laughing. Dedalus snarled at them and beached the boat. He led Andy away from the shore.

"You watch yourself, young Icarus!" called one of the men.

In the depths of Andy's memory, the small bell began to ring more loudly.

"Icarus and Dedalus?" Suddenly, the bell started ringing like a fire alarm. "Oh no," he groaned.

Andy had met mythological creatures before. They kept turning up like uninvited guests at a party. But they had always come to his world. This time, it looked as though he might have gone back in time to . . . No, it was impossible. Surely he couldn't have.

Dedalus stopped at a long, low building and threw open a pair of rickety wooden doors. Andy peered inside and gave a gasp of astonishment. In the gloom, he could make out a long table standing in the centre of the room. Lying on it were two huge frames, one of which was partly covered in feathers. Andy realised that he was looking at a gigantic pair of half-finished wings; but they didn't look anything like the cutaway sections of wings Andy had seen in books, with spars and ribs. They were made out of some kind of thin, strong wood, woven like a basket.

"Get to work!" Dedalus pointed at the wings. "And for your own sake, make sure you do a good job."

"Why for my sake?" quavered Andy.

"Because you'll be wearing them," snarled Dedalus, "next time you jump off the cliff . . ."

Chapter Four

PILOT ERROR

Eddie gazed at Perce in horror. "You mean . . . we're getting dragged into another Greek myth?"

"It looks like it," said Perce wearily.

"So who is this geezer?" Well'ard jerked a grimy thumb at Icarus. "One of your mythological mates, is he?"

Perce gave him a scornful glance. "Even you must have heard of the Legend of Icarus."

"Why must I? I only like legends with fighting in."

Well'ard leapt off the bench and delivered a devastating Ninja attack on a litter bin.

Eddie shook his head. "But why didn't Mr Latimer spot that it wasn't Andy in the pool?"

Perce shrugged. 'It's happened before. Don't you remember? With Ms Dusa, for instance. Kids were being turned to stone, and nobody even noticed that anything weird was going on. I think something happens when characters from myths start getting into our world. People get confused about what is real and what isn't."

Eddie thought hard. "You mean, when things start happening that shouldn't be happening, people pretend they aren't happening because it's easier to do that than work out what *is* happening."

Well'ard said, "I was with you right up to when you said, 'You mean' . . ."

Perce groaned. "Well'ard, a sleeping policeman's got more brains than you have. Listen, remember when we got in the Labyrinth?"

Well'ard shuddered and Eddie turned pale; they weren't likely to forget the terrifying maze in which the Minotaur (half man, half bull and all trouble) lived.

"Well, Dedalus . . . his dad . . ." Perce pointed at Icarus. "He built the Labyrinth for King Minos."

Well'ard gave Icarus a knowing look. "Oh, did he? Must have been worth a bit of money, a big contract like that."

Icarus looked uncomfortable. "Not exactly. As soon as my father had finished building the Labyrinth, King Minos threw him into prison."

"Tough cheddar," said Well'ard cheerfully. "Made a bodge of it, did he?"

Perce shook her head. "When Theseus went to Crete to fight the Minotaur, Dedalus helped Theseus and Ariadne find their way through the maze."

Eddie nodded. "You can see Minos would be a bit narked about that. It's like somebody selling you a really expensive bike lock, and then going and giving the combination to every bike-thief in town."

"Eventually, Minos let my father out of prison, but he wouldn't let us leave." Icarus sighed. "Crete is an island, so the only way to get off was by sea, and Minos had all the ports watched. But my father thought of another way to escape."

Perce looked at him steadily. "He decided you could both fly away from Crete."

Icarus gave her a startled look. "How do you know?"

"Well, you see . . ." Perce bit her lip. Talking to Icarus wasn't like talking to Andy, or Eddie, or Well'ard. He didn't seem as stupid, and Perce had a vague feeling that she didn't want to upset him. This was odd, because upsetting boys was one of Perce's chief pleasures in life.

She tried again. "You see, all this stuff with you and your dad . . . it all happened a long time ago. So long ago that people aren't sure whether it really happened or not. It's a legend, to us."

"The Legend of Icarus," said Eddie. "That sounds familiar." He began to go cross-eyed with the effort of remembering.

"We've had visits from . . . people from legends before." Perce didn't somehow feel this was quite the moment to tell Icarus that their earlier visitors had generally wanted to get rid of her and Andy in various nasty ways. "We don't even know exactly where they come from, whether it's the past . . . our past, I mean . . . or whether there's a sort of

34

World of Myth where things are . . . well, different," she finished lamely.

Icarus thought for a moment, and then said, "This legend you're talking about . . ." He hesitated. "Does it have a . . . happy ending?"

Perce felt her mouth going dry. "Why do you ask?"

"It's just that my father's plans haven't worked very well. I've tried lots of wings for him, and none of them work. Every time, he says that I must jump from a higher place so the wings have more time to work." He looked up at Perce. "I thought I was going to die when I fell today. Sooner or later . . ."

"Got it!" Eddie snapped his fingers. "I do know this one! You see, what happens is, your dad makes these wings that *do* work, and you fly off over the sea . . ."

"Eddie," hissed Perce warningly.

". . . only you fly too close to the sun, and the wax holding the feathers on your wings melts . . ."

"Eddie, shut up!"

" . . . and you fall in the sea and drown." Eddie looked from Icarus's stricken face to Perce's vicious scowl. "Was it something I said?"

Perce turned to Icarus. "Don't worry, it's not going to happen." She realised she was gabbling and forced herself to speak calmly. "It's just a story. Anyway, nothing like that can happen to you while you're here, can it?"

"It can to Andy though." There was an odd quiver in Eddie's voice. "If Icarus has come out of the legend and turned up here, then this Dedalus bloke is going to be looking for a new test-pilot isn't he? And if you two are right and Andy has gone into the legend . . ."

Perce groaned and collapsed onto the bench. "Then it will be Andy who falls into the sea and drowns!"

Chapter Five

FLIGHT PLAN

The problem of finding Icarus somewhere to stay had been solved quite simply. Perce had walked Icarus back to Andy's house. When she had opened the door, Andy's mum had looked surprised for a moment; but then Perce had pushed Icarus into the house, and called out "Goodnight, Andy," and that had been that.

"She stared at me a few times," Icarus told Perce that morning as they walked to school. "She looked a bit puzzled, but after a while she seemed just to . . . accept me." He shrugged.

The first session for Perce's class was science. As luck would have it, the current topic was flight. Although he'd missed the first week of the project, Icarus was fascinated by Mr Latimer's explanation about wing shapes.

Soon, his hand was in the air. "Excuse me, please," he said. "Are you saying that a wing has to be curved before it will work?"

Mr Latimer gave a long-suffering sigh. "Andrew, we covered all this last week."

Icarus realized that he had come close to giving the game away. "I am sorry," he said hurriedly, "I must have forgotten."

"Then for the benefit of Andrew – and anyone else who was not paying attention . . ." Mr Latimer swept his eyes across the class, all of whom tried to look as if not paying attention was the furthest thing from their minds. ". . . I shall explain the basic principles of aerodynamics once again." He tapped a diagram with his board marker. "The curve of an aircraft wing is designed to make the air pressure underneath of the wing greater than that on top. Therefore, when the wing is moving forwards and air is flowing over it, the difference in pressure creates lift . . ."

Icarus followed the explanation carefully and watched a DVD about gliding with shining eyes.

At break, Perce found that it was Mr Latimer's turn to supervise the detention.

"Sit down, Priscilla!"

Perce squirmed inside. She hated to be called by her real name, but she arranged her face in a sweet smile (Look Number Three for dealing with teachers: "*Open and Innocent*").

"And what are you grinning like that for? You look like a blasted gargoyle." Mr Latimer was missing his morning snack. His hands were twitching: a sure sign of Bikkie Withdrawal Syndrome, thought Perce. Anyway, look who was calling her a gargoyle! She let the smile fade and tried Look Number Seven, "*Serious and Attentive*".

"Please, sir . . ."

"Have you brought any work to do? If not, I'm sure I can find you some."

"Yes I have sir," lied Perce. "I've brought my science project. The one we're doing on aero-thingy . . . you know, sir, flying."

"Aerodynamics."

"Yes, sir, only I need some help."

Mr Latimer wasn't feeling helpful. He didn't want to supervise Perce, who was the only pupil on punishment. He wanted to be in the staffroom with a nice cup of coffee and a chocolate digestive. "If you need to know something, you'll have to look it up."

Old misery, thought Perce. Aloud, she said, "But I'm not allowed out of the punishment room, sir."

Mr Latimer groaned. "Go on, then."

"Well, sir, is it possible for people to fly? I mean, not in a plane or anything, just fly by themselves?"

"No."

Perce waited patiently. She knew Mr Latimer wouldn't be able to leave it at that; he was a teacher, after all. Teachers needed to explain things.

"Well, people can glide of course, with the right equipment, but they have to start from somewhere high up. But real flying . . . no. People are too heavy. Their muscles aren't strong enough."

"But what about Icarus, sir? He flew, didn't he?"

"Poppycock!" Mr Latimer tended to get over-heated when discussing Greek Myths. "That's just a legend. Firstly, in real life, Icarus and Dedalus would never have got off the ground. Secondly, if Icarus had flown towards the sun, the air would have got colder as he gained height, not hotter, so the wax on his wings wouldn't have melted . . ." he stopped and threw Perce a suspicious glance. "Why this sudden interest in mythology, anyway? Nothing's . . . happened, has it?"

"Oh no, sir," lied Perce with a bright smile. "Nothing at all."

Dedalus's workshop was hopelessly cluttered. Strange looking tools lay where they had been dropped. Dozens of clay pots, hundreds of pieces of metal, string and rope were scattered about, filling the room from floor to ceiling. It looked like a scrap yard after a hurricane.

Dedalus dug a double handful of feathers from a bag in the corner, sneezed violently, and shambled over to where Andy sat slumped in exhaustion.

"Come on, then! What are you waiting for?" The

old man put the feathers down, crossed to his fire, and lifted a pot of newly melted wax from it. He brought it over to Andy. "The wings, boy, the wings!"

Andy looked at the wings in confusion. "But I've finished them, haven't I? I mean there aren't any gaps or anything . . ."

"Oh, yes!" roared Dedalus, "you'd like that, wouldn't you! One pair of wings! One! So you can fly off and leave your old Dad behind, is that the idea? Oh no, my boy . . ." With an effort, Dedalus lifted the finished wings off the table. "We go together!"

Stacking the feathered wings against the wall, the old man took down a second set of woven frames. Andy gazed at them in horror. It had taken him most of the night to finish the first set! As Dedalus lifted the new frames onto the table, there was a terrific banging at the door. Someone outside bellowed, "Open! In the name of King Minos!"

Dedalus gave a gasp of terror. All the bad temper and bluster seemed to drain out of him. He scuttled over to the door and opened it, practically groveling to the two men who came in. They were big men with jaws like anvils. They wore armour and carried spears.

They looked around the workshop while Dedalus bowed and cringed. One of them turned suddenly and thrust the point of his spear to within a centimetre of Dedalus's nose. The old man went cross-eyed staring at the sharp tip.

The soldier with the spear said, "King Minos is very disappointed."

The other soldier said, "Yeah, disappointed."

"He only let you out of the Labyrinth," the first soldier went on, "because you promised to build him a flying ship . . ."

"Yeah, ship."

". . . and that was weeks ago, so now he wants to know, what's the holdup?"

"Yeah, holdup?"

Dedalus waved his hands about. "Boys, boys, I promise you, I'm working on it, these things take time! I did a test just yesterday . . ."

"And did it work?"

"Yeah, work?"

"Well, not exactly, but next time . . ."

The man with the spear moved his lips. He may

have thought he was smiling. "Next time, it'd better work. King Minos says you got two days. If you're not ready by then . . ." he made a throat-cutting gesture, ". . . you'll be for the high jump. Geddit? High jump!" He roared with laughter.

"Yeah, the long jump. Hur hur hur."

The first soldier stopped laughing and gave the second a dirty look. "Long jump? Are you stupid?"

"Yeah, stupid."

"Come on!"

The two soldiers went out, breaking a few things on the way.

Dedalus shut the door behind them, and leaned against it, panting. "Get to work! You heard them. If we're not ready in two days, they'll throw us both off the cliff!" He glared at Andy. "Without wings!"

Chapter Six

A TOUCH OF FLEW

Eddie rocked gently back and forth on a swing. "I've got a plan," he chirped.

"Oh yeah?" sneered Perce.

"Yeah. Simple. We think Andy went back to where Icarus came from when he came here, so all we've got to do is find some way to send Icarus back from here to there at the same time as bringing Andy back from there to here, if he's there in the first place!"

"Nice plan," replied Perce sarcastically. "How do we do that, then?"

"I haven't thought of that bit yet. Give me a chance!"

Perce looked at Icarus. "Anyway, we can't send Icarus back."

Well'ard sat on the monkey bars scratching his head, making several fleas homeless. "Why not?" he asked. "Anyway, why do *we* have to think of a plan? Why can't the Greek geek over there come up with one?"

Perce clenched her fists. "He's not a geek. And we can't send him back, because his dad will kill him with his daft inventions. Anyway, he's not like the other mythological nutters we've met. He's nice and . . ." Perce tailed off as Well'ard and Eddie stared hard at her.

"You fancy 'im!" hooted Well'ard.

"No, I don't," denied Perce.

"Yes you do! You're going red!"

Perce felt a blush spreading over her cheeks. "I must be coming down with flu," she muttered lamely.

"Perhaps you caught it off him," said Eddie pointing at Icarus. "He 'flu' here!"

Well'ard and Eddie both fell about barking with laughter.

Perce felt embarrassed. Why shouldn't she like Icarus? For a boy, he was all right. Mind you, she'd never let on that she thought so. Not to anyone. No way!

Eddie took a break from barking like a demented seal to whisper in Well'ard's ear. Well'ard began to guffaw and nodded at Eddie.

"Hey, Perce what are your favourite sweets?" Eddie asked innocently.

"Why?"

"I bet they're . . . Icarus Allsorts!" Eddie and Well'ard fell about in even greater fits of laughter.

"Right! Enough's enough!" Perce grabbed Eddie by his collar and put her fist up against his mouth. "Actually Eddie, my favourite sweets are *gobstoppers*! Now, are you going to cut out the stupid comments?"

Eddie and Well'ard nodded dumbly. This was more like the Perce they knew and loved – well at least, knew.

"Now," said Perce calmly, "we need a proper

plan."

"Why don't we ask Liquorice?" asked Well'ard. "Maybe he's got a plan."

Icarus looked up. "I think I shall need my wings."

"But they're broken," protested Perce. "Anyway, I told you, I asked Latimer and he says people can't fly."

"Not here, they can't." Eddie thought hard. "Where Icarus comes from, it might be different. If there are creatures that can turn people to stone, or are half human and half bull, flying should be a doddle!"

Perce nodded decisively. "In that case, we'll have to build some new wings. What are they made of?"

"Steel," said Well'ard confidently.

"Well'ard, how can you be so stupid with only one head? We're not talking about aeroplane wings!"

Icarus spoke up. "My father makes wings from wooden frames covered with feathers."

Well'ard grinned. "I know where we can get some feathers."

"Good." Perce pointed at Well'ard. "You and Eddie go and get them. Icarus and I will sort out the frames. And hurry! Andy could be in terrible danger."

"He'll be all right," said Eddie, trying to reassure everyone. "He's probably having a great time, lazing about on a beach getting a nice sun tan or something . . ."

"Get a move on you idle creature, or I'll flog you until your back bleeds!" Dedalus was standing over Andy holding a thick cane.

"Why have I got to do all the work?" Andy asked, picking up a pile of feathers.

"Because, ah . . . aah . . . aaah aaaachoo! Because I'm allergic to feathers. I sneeze and come out in rashes."

"Well I'm allergic to work," muttered Andy, "I yawn and come out in tiredness."

"Don't be insolent, boy!" boomed Dedalus. "You heard King Minos' men – we only have two more days to build his ship."

"But you're not building a ship!"

"Exactly, that's why we have to build the wings, leap off the cliff and fly to our freedom before they return. Achoo!"

Andy looked down at the wings. He'd been sticking feathers onto the frames for hours. I wish I had a tube of super glue, he thought.

Dedalus looked carefully at Andy's work. "This side of the frame is covered. We need to turn the wing over. Help me lift it . . ."

Andy's jaw dropped. Inspiration hit him like a snowball down the earhole. That was what was wrong! That's why Dedalus's wings wouldn't work.

"Lift!" he shouted. "That's it! Lift!"

Dedalus stared at him. "Yes . . . lift. Pick . . . It . . . Up . . . And . . . Lift."

"No, I mean that's what you need. That's why you haven't been able to fly. The wings should be curved, like a bird's. That's what gives them lift."

Dedalus shook his head. "Mad. The boy's gone mad."

"No, I haven't! These wings are straight. The aerodynamics are wrong."

Dedalus looked puzzled. "The hairy dry maniacs? What are they?"

"Aerodynamics . . . they're . . . dynamics . . . of air." Andy wished he hadn't fallen asleep during that bit of Mr Latimer's lesson.

Dedalus spluttered with rage. "Are you trying to tell me, the greatest inventor the world has ever seen, that you know more about the science of flight than I do?"

"We're doing it at school."

"School? What's school?"

Andy realised that schools hadn't been invented yet. Well'ard should be here, he thought, he'd be in heaven!

"It doesn't matter. The wings have got to be curved." Dedalus shook his head angrily. "Look," Andy went on, "even if I'm wrong, nothing you've tried so far has worked. What have you got to lose?"

Dedalus stood in silence for a long time, biting his lip. Eventually he spread his hands. "All right. Curved. We'll try it." He glowered at Andy. "So you'd better get working even harder. We must be ready to escape."

Andy nodded. "I'm right about the curved wings. You'll see."

"Oh, I shall." Dedalus gave him a wicked grin. "Because when we jump off the cliff, you go first."

Chapter Seven

FEATHERED FRIENDS

"Are you sure this will work?" asked Eddie as he watched Well'ard ripping up pieces of bread and throwing them on the ground. The trail of bread led from the park lake to a large clump of bushes.

"'Course it will," replied Well'ard. "The stupid ducks will eat the bread and then we nab 'em with this." He held up a landing net which he had nicked from his dad's fishing kit. "The SAS do this to survive in the desert," he continued.

Eddie rolled his eyes. Well'ard's one ambition in life was to get into the Special Air Service. "But there aren't any ducks in the desert," he pointed out.

"That's cos the SAS caught them all." Well'ard threw down the last scrap of bread and settled himself in a large rhododendron bush. "You doubtin' me?"

"No . . ." said Eddie, doubting him.

"Well, come 'ere and get ready to pluck duck!"

For the next hour Eddie crouched next to Well'ard, ready to grab any unsuspecting ducks that had taken the bait. His fingers ached from gripping the landing net and cramp had begun to set in his leg.

"How long do we have to wait?" he hissed.

"For as long as it takes." Well'ard's face was set hard with determination. "Sometimes the SAS wait for days."

"But I've got to be home for tea . . ."

"Wimp! You'd never survive in the desert."

"I'm not in the desert. I'm in a bush in the park . . ."

"Shhh!" hissed Well'ard. "Hear that?" There was

a scratching noise coming from round the corner. "We've got one!" Well'ard's voice squeaked in excitement. "Get the net ready."

Eddie obeyed and raised the net.

"Come on duck . . ." whispered Well'ard, eyes ablaze with anticipation.

"Sniff, sniff."

A seed of doubt began to grow in Eddie's mind. "Sniff, sniff?" He was sure ducks didn't sniff.

"Well'ard . . .?"

"Shhhh! Get ready . . ."

"But . . ." The seed had grown into a medium-sized garden centre.

"SSHHHH! It's nearly here . . . ready, Eddie . . . GO!"

Well'ard and Eddie leapt out and threw the net.

After a moment's pause, Eddie said in a very flat sort of voice, "Well'ard . . . you know about ducks, don't you?"

"Erm . . . yeah."

"Are there any ducks that have fur?"

"Erm . . ."

"Are there any ducks that growl?"

"Well . . ."

"Are there any ducks that are as big as a sheep and have got four legs and very large teeth?"

"Ah . . . no."

"Then I think what we've got here is an Alsatian."

"GRRRRRRR . . ."

"RUN!"

An hour later Well'ard and Eddie were back at the side of the lake. Their clothes were tattered from their encounter with the four legged, bushy tailed 'duck'. Nevertheless, a few scratches, bite marks and torn clothes weren't enough to deter Well'ard. He eyed the ducks happily swimming on the lake.

"Right, time for Plan B."

Eddie rubbed his backside. "I hope its better than Plan A. That dog bit me right on the . . ."

"Stop moaning," ordered Well'ard. "This time we creep up on that load of ducks."

"Flock."

"What?"

"You mean a flock of ducks. It's a collective noun," explained Eddie.

Well'ard just stood staring blankly.

"It's a term given to the name of a group of

things," continued Eddie.

Well'ard continued staring blankly.

"For instance, you have a herd of cattle or a flight of birds . . . a brood of chickens . . ."

"Eddie, shut it."

". . . a shrewdness of apes . . . an unkindness of ravens . . . a murder of crows . . ."

Well'ard grabbed Eddie's torn collar.

"If you don't shut it, there will be an unkindness of me and a murder of Eddie."

Eddie shut up.

"Right. We'll have that one." Well'ard pointed to a duck which had wandered away from the lake and was nonchalantly pecking at the grass. "It's duck pluckin' time!"

Eddie watched as Well'ard took what was left of the landing net and began to tiptoe towards the duck.

"Here ducky, ducky," Well'ard whispered, "Come to uncle Well'ard . . ."

Eddie held his breath as Well'ard got closer to the duck, which ignored him.

"Verzoooing!" Well'ard held the net like a light sabre. His breath became rasping. "Hurr-haaa . . .

hurr-haaa . . . The force is strong with this one."

The duck stopped pecking at the ground. Well'ard stopped dead in his tracks. "*Hasta la vista*, ducky!"

The duck turned and, instead of flying off, craned its neck, beat its wings and advanced on the two 'hunters'.

"Er . . . what's up, duck?"

"QUACK!"

"RUN!"

"Plan C is bound to work."

Eddie was not convinced. He and Well'ard had returned to the lake after being chased across the park by the mad duck and its mates. Their clothes were even more tattered.

"What's plan C?" asked Eddie.

"We forget the creeping up bit. Look, there's a duck just the other side of those bushes. You can see its feathers."

Eddie was too battered and bruised to argue. He just nodded his head weakly.

"So what we do is, we dive through the bushes and grab it before it knows what's happenin'. Surprise attack, right? One, two, three . . ."

They dived through the bushes. Well'ard reached out blindly, grabbed and yanked hard. He held up his hand in triumph.

"Free!" he gloated. "I got free feathers . . ."

"Well'ard . . ."

Well'ard turned. Eddie was standing stock still and pointing a trembling finger.

"That isn't a duck. That's a swan."

Well'ard eyed the large white form. "So? It's still got feathers."

"A swan can break a person's arm with its wing," quivered Eddie as he slowly backed away. "Swans are vicious. Especially when they get annoyed."

"Do you reckon it looks annoyed?" asked Well'ard.

"You've just pulled three feathers off its bum! What do you think?"

"HISS!"

"RUN!"

"Three feathers! Is that all you've got? We need thousands!"

Perce was unimpressed by Well'ard and Eddie's adventures. Even Icarus had laughed at their description of the attack of the killer duck.

"You ran away from a duck?" sneered Perce. "Was it a well'ard mallard?"

"It bit me," protested Well'ard.

"Ducks don't have teeth, they have bills."

"All right, it *billed* me then."

Perce shook her head. "Pathetic, absolutely pathetic."

"Well," huffed Eddie, "If you're going to be like that you can get your own feathers."

Well'ard nodded in agreement.

"Come Well'ard, we're obviously not wanted here." Eddie stalked off. "I have a better idea. I know how we can save Andy . . ."

Chapter Eight

BIRD BRAINS

Icarus finished tightening a screw and stepped back to admire his handiwork. "Done!"

He and Perce had spent the whole of Saturday in Perce's garage working on the new wings. The frame of the left hand wing lay across the workbench. The right hand frame lay wobbling across the handle of the lawnmower and the back of a folding garden chair. Perce glued another feather onto it, then turned round.

They were working from plans for a flying model aeroplane kit (which Perce's dad had bought but never found the time to make up). Once Icarus had got the idea from the drawings, there had been no stopping him. All the tools in the garage were unfamiliar to him, especially the powered ones, but he was a quick learner. Before long he was exclaiming delightedly at the speed with which the electric saw cut shapes out of plywood (which Perce's dad had bought for some do-it-yourself work in the loft). The first frame had been completed using thin strips of wood and covered with shade netting.

"Oh goodie. Another wing to cover." Perce turned back to her work and carefully glued another feather onto the frame. "Seven thousand, four hundred and thirty three," she said wearily. She picked up another feather and dabbed a spot of glue on the end. "Seven thousand, four hundred and . . ."

Icarus came and looked over her shoulder. "We should be using wax," he complained.

Perce shook her head. "You can't get hold of wax that easily these days, not unless you fancy digging around in Well'ard's ears. Anyway, this is the latest stuff. Sticks anything. And it won't melt if it gets hot."

"Where did you get the feathers from, anyway?"

"You don't want to know."

"Yes I do. That's why I asked."

"When I say you don't want to know," Perce explained, "I mean you may want to know, but if you did know, you'd wish you didn't. Believe me, you *really* don't want to know."

As Icarus was still trying to puzzle this out, a thunderous banging shook the garage door. Perce went across and opened it. Outside, Eddie and Well'ard were leaning on their bikes.

"What do you want?" demanded Perce sourly. "I thought you weren't helping any more."

"Well, that's all you know, see," sneered Well'ard. "We ain't been wasting our time like you have. We done the business."

Eddie was beside himself excitement. "Come on!" He grabbed Perce by the sleeve. "We've got something to show you."

Perce shook him off. "What could you bozos have to show us?"

Well'ard waved his hand in the air. "Only the answer to all your boyfriend's problems . . ."

"He is *not* my boyfr . . ."

"Only the thing that's going to get Andy back." Well'ard looked even more smug. "Job done. Sorted!"

Perce put her hands on her hips. "Listen, you turkeys, if you think I'm going to drop everything and get roped in to one of your hare-brained schemes . . ."

"PERCE!"

". . . you're absolutely right!" Perce grabbed her bike and leapt on it. As she pedalled furiously away, she could still hear her mother calling after her . . .

"Perce! Where are you going? Have you seen my best duvet? The feather one? I can't find it anywhere . . ."

Perce gazed at the contraption. "What is it?"

"Hang glider," said Eddie proudly. "Me and Well'ard made it."

"Yeah," smirked Well'ard. "While you an' lover-boy were messin' about with feathers, we built this. Took us nearly all night."

Perce leant on her handlebars. She hadn't much idea what went into the construction of a hang glider, but she was pretty sure it didn't include a clothes horse, aluminium curtain track or nasty pink nylon bedsheets. Eddie's creation looked like a kite that had crashed into a television aerial.

Icarus stood beside Perce, panting. He had some excuse: he didn't have a bike, and had run all the way. "What is it?" he asked. "A windmill?"

Perce turned to stare at Eddie. "I thought you said you had a plan to save Andy."

"We have!" Eddie was indignant. "All Liquorice has got to do is strap himself in here and put on the rollerblades, get up a bit of speed down the hill, and hey presto!"

"Yeah, hey presto, sudden death. Eddie, you're out of your tree."

"Come on, there's nothing to worry about." Eddie reached inside his backpack and pulled out a flying helmet and a pair of goggles. He offered them to Icarus, who shook his head and backed away.

"Tell you what," said Perce. "You show us."

Eddie gulped. "Me?"

Perce and Icarus watched with interest as Eddie and Well'ard went through the final pre-flight checks.

"Contact!"

"Contact who?" asked Eddie. "You mean, phone them or something?"

Well'ard looked baffled. "I dunno, it's just what they say in films before they take off."

Eddie straightened his goggles. "Okay, what's next?"

"Chocks away!" Well'ard reached into Eddie's pocket and whipped out a Chocolate Yummy Bar.

"Hey, what are you doing with that?"

"Well, you don't want it to get squashed, do you?"

"Look, I'm not sure this is such a good idea . . ."

"Wilco! Roger! Over and out!" Well'ard gave Eddie a good hard shove. With a stifled squeak, Eddie the Eagle set off down the runway.

The rollerblades rumbled on the tarmac road surface. Eddie's contraption swayed and wobbled alarmingly. Bits began to flap loose.

Hopping up and down in excitement, Well'ard cupped his hands in front of his mouth and yelled,

"Rotate!"

Eddie was really getting up speed now. From far away, they heard him scream:

"What? Turn round, at this speed? You must be mad!"

"It means take off!" bellowed Well'ard. "Take off!"

Perce and Icarus watched open-mouthed as Eddie's feet left the ground . . .

Chapter Nine

FLIGHTS OF FANCY

Andy snored. He was asleep on a pile of feathers. They weren't as comfortable as they looked. They tickled.

He and Dedalus had spent most of the night trying to put a curve in the wings. Eventually, Dedalus had decided that the easiest way to do this was to soak the wings, and bend them while they were wet. This had meant several trips down to the beach, carrying the wings to dip them in the sea.

Also, most of the feathers had come off in the water, and had to be collected. Andy had fallen asleep while Dedalus was working on the frames.

"Wake up, you idle dog!"

A vicious kick sent Andy sprawling. He looked up to see Dedalus standing over him, scowling.

"What was that for?" he complained.

"You haven't time to lie about!" Dedalus jerked his thumb at the wings. Andy looked at them, and groaned.

A few pitiful feathers still clung to the frames, but the rest were lying in scattered heaps round the workshop, wet and bedraggled.

Dedalus kicked Andy again. "Get back to work. All these feathers – Achoo! – have got to be dried. Then you've got two pairs of wings to cover."

Andy groaned. "I'm sick of sticking feathers! I don't care if the stupid wings never get finished."

"Would you rather be hurled from a terrible height and fall screaming to a horrific death on jagged rocks?"

Andy thought for a moment. "Good point, well made." He reached for the pot of wax.

Eddie took to the air. He sailed over a hedge. Defying gravity, he rose like a swan, he swooped like a falcon . . .

. . . he dropped like a brick.

Eddie came to earth with the sort of noise you might get if you had an attack of wind while sitting in a bath full of yoghurt.

As Well'ard set off down the hill at a sprint, Perce plucked a blade of grass and chewed it. "Good job the farmer decided to put his manure pile just there. Nice soft landing. Mind you, it looks a bit squishy."

Icarus looked concerned. "Do you think we should help them?" he asked, without enthusiasm.

"Nah."

At the bottom of the hill, Well'ard was trying to pull Eddie from the heap by his feet. He was finding this difficult as he was trying to hold his nose at the same time.

Perce turned her bike round with a sigh. "Come on. We'd better get back to gluing feathers. Maybe mum will have calmed down a bit by now . . ."
She suddenly became aware that Icarus hadn't moved. A shadow passed over her. She turned.

Icarus was staring up into the sky, entranced.

Perce looked up. A hang-glider soared effortlessly across the face of the hill. Catching an updraft, it began to climb in a lazy spiral. Icarus stared at it with longing in his eyes.

"It can be done," he whispered. "Human beings can fly."

Perce put down her bike and stood beside him. "You remember Latimer going on about warm air currents? – whadjamacallums, thermals. That glider pilot has found one. He's using it to gain height. That's the secret. You don't fight the wind, you use it." She watched the glider climb steadily. "They don't often come over here – he must have flown miles!"

Icarus licked his lips. "With one of those, I could jump off the highest cliff with no fear. I could escape from Crete. I could escape from my father!"

Perce shook her head regretfully. "Forget it. They cost thousands of pounds."

Icarus looked crestfallen.

Shielding her eyes, Perce gazed towards the distant hills where the hang gliders launched. She could just make out two or three of the graceful swallow-winged shapes . . . and a dumpier, mushroom shaped wing some way below them that seemed to swing like a pendulum. That would be a paraglider. A parachute you could fly like a glider. A parachute . . .

"Yes!" Perce punched the air. Icarus turned a startled face to her. "Listen, no time to explain. Help Well'ard get Eddie out. Get them both to help you finish the wings. See you later."

Pedalling furiously, Perce covered the ten miles to the local airfield in forty minutes.

The instructor from the parachute training school rubbed his chin. "Well, I dunno. For school, you said?"

Perce held her breath. She knew that the drama club at the comprehensive school had a parachute. They had brought it to Perce's school for a workshop.

"What school is it?"

Perce told him. The instructor brightened. "Hey, yeah? Is old Latimer still there?"

"Er . . . yes."

"He used to be my teacher. I reckon it was him

that got me interested in skydiving. I mean, after you've been hauled over the coals a few times by old Latimer, jumping out of an aeroplane at seventeen thousand feet doesn't seem like any big deal."

Perce nodded. She knew what he meant.

"I think I can do something for you. We've got a few old 'chutes we were going to hire out to a film company, but the film got cancelled." The instructor disappeared into a store-room and came out carrying something that looked like a floppy rucksack. "Well, this one's all packed up and ready to go. We're sending the old stuff out to schools and charities next week, but you can have it now if you like. Are you going to do some drama with it, then?"

Perce picked up the pack and smiled. "If things work out all right, I reckon it could be pretty dramatic."

Chapter Ten

FLY AWAY HOME

The following evening, Perce peered cautiously through the doorway from the changing room. The pool was deserted.

She had hidden in a cubicle until the changing rooms emptied when the pool closed. Now she crept round the edge of the pool to the fire exit, opened it and whistled.

Eddie and Well'ard scampered out from the bushes carrying the finished wings. Icarus followed more slowly with a large bundle. Perce pulled the fire door shut behind them.

"Right," she hissed, "they'll be turning the alarms on in a few minutes. Let's get cracking." Icarus looked around, undecided. "Look, you'll have the parachute. It'll work. Trust me."

Icarus gazed at her for a moment, then nodded and started to peel off the tracksuit he'd borrowed from Andy's wardrobe. At a signal from Perce, Eddie (who still niffed a bit from yesterday's crash landing) and Well'ard started to climb the steps to the top diving board, hauling the wings up with them.

Finishing the wings had taken the whole day, even with all four of them gluing feathers. The results were pretty impressive. The wings were light, and seemed strong enough. They looked terrific; but would they fly?

Perce lifted the pack onto Icarus's back, and helped him adjust the harness. "This is the rip-cord. Pull it if the wings don't work, and the para-chute will open out."

Icarus nodded.

"If the wings do work, then you can still use the

parachute to get away from your father. You climb as high as you can, and . . ."

"Yes, I remember. It's a good plan. Thank you."

Well'ard appeared at Perce's elbow. "We put the wings on the platform. All he's gotta do is strap 'em on and jump off yelling 'Bonsai!'"

Perce rolled her eyes. "Banzai."

"Whatever. Shall we help him get the wings on?"

"I'll do it. You watch the doors."

"Want to give him a goodbye kissy-wissy, do you?" Well'ard saw Perce's fists clench. "Tell you what, I'll watch the doors."

Perce turned to Icarus. "Come on."

They started to climb towards the diving platform.

Andy stood on top of the cliff. The afternoon sun beat down on him. He shivered. How had he got into this mess? What was he doing here? Why didn't he just run away?

He felt the point of Dedalus's dagger jab into his back. Ah yes, that was the reason.

Dedalus's harsh voice grated in his ear. "What are you waiting for? Jump!"

Andy looked down. He felt his head swimming. Far, far below, the sea crashed onto wicked-looking rocks. "Look, the doctor says I mustn't go jumping off cliffs because it might bring on a nasty attack of getting killed, also I've got a verucca, my Mum gave me a note . . ."

"Stop your foul whining!" Dedalus brought his knife up to Andy's throat. "Jump!"

"After you."

Dedalus snorted. "You cry baby! What are you making such a fuss about? It's one small step for a man . . ."

"No it isn't! It's a giant leap with lots of 'aaarrrgh' and a 'splat' at the end!"

The knife hovered a millimetre from Andy's belly button. "If you don't jump, the crows shall feast on your living entrails."

"Well, since you ask so nicely . . ." Andy gulped. He spread his wings and stepped off the cliff. "Mummmmmmeeeeeeeeeee!"

Out of control, with wings flapping madly, Andy hurtled towards certain death on the rocks below.

Perce pulled the last strap on the wings tight. She

glanced down at the unnaturally clear and glassy surface of the empty pool. "That's it, then. Remember, don't fight the air. Use it." She looked up. Icarus was staring straight into her eyes.

Perce suddenly felt very hot and very small.

"Look, maybe this isn't such a good idea," she said in a slightly shaky voice. "Perhaps there's another way of getting Andy back . . ."

"No. This is the only way." Icarus looked at her steadily. "Thank you for all you've done."

"But what if the wings don't work? What if . . .?"

"If the wings don't work, maybe the parachute will." Icarus shrugged. "I think I have a much better chance now than I did when I came here. What happens, the gods will decide."

He paused, and smiled slightly. Then he leant forward, just a little.

He's going to kiss me, thought Perce. Hooray! Help!

She closed her eyes.

When she opened them again, Icarus was gone.

Chapter Eleven

SPLASHDOWN

It seemed to Icarus that a thousand stars had exploded and lit up every corner of his brain. He screwed his eyes shut. When they blinked open, the harsh neon light of the swimming pool had been transformed into bright blinding sunlight. As he tumbled helplessly through the air, Icarus glimpsed the figure of his father peering over the edge of the cliff. The plan had worked, he was back!

The feeling of relief quickly vanished as Icarus

realised he was plunging towards the rocks below. He began to panic and tried to flap his arms. It was no good, he couldn't! His wings were being pushed upwards by the force of the air. He was going to die.

A huge splash echoed round the pool.

Perce half ran, half slid down the steps from the diving board. She reached the poolside. Eddie and Well'ard stood gazing dumbly at the water. Waves splashed over their feet. The whole surface of the pool was smothered with feathers.

Perce grabbed the long pole that the instructors used to tow beginners. She fished around under the surface and felt the pole poke into something soft.

With an eruption of feathers, a head broke the surface. Well'ard and Eddie burst into loud cheers. Perce breathed a sigh of relief. "Welcome back Andy." She put her hands on her hips. "Well? Are you going to splash around enjoying yourself all day?"

By the time the piggy-eyed attendant arrived, his howls of rage echoed round a deserted pool.

Thousands of feathers danced on its ruffled surface, and an open fire door swung gently in the breeze.

As Icarus closed his eyes and waited for the inevitable sickening crunch, a familiar female voice from across the centuries seemed to whisper in his ear.

"*Don't fight the air. Use it.*"

With a muscle-wrenching effort, Icarus pulled his arms down and held them out horizontally. Spray from the crashing waves stung his face. The rocks got nearer and nearer as Icarus stretched out for his life and shouted out Perce's advice.

"Don't fight the air! USE IT!"

As if obeying his demand, air billowed under the wings and lifted Icarus out of the death dive. He began to glide up and away from the body-tearing waves and brain-splitting rocks.

He was doing it! He was flying!

"It works!" Icarus heard his father's triumphant cry from the cliff top. "I knew it would! I am a genius!"

Icarus soared gleefully along the cliff edge. All

right, Father, he thought. It's your turn to jump now, see how you like it. Let's see you fly. And then . . . catch me if you can. He laughed out loud. His wings carried him aloft like a bird . . . no, like a god! He was invincible! He could do anything! Dedalus watched Icarus soaring away, gliding and swooping on the currents of hot air.

"Well done, my boy! Farewell, Minos! Farewell, Crete!" chuckled Dedalus as he strapped on his pair of wings and made his way to the cliff's edge. He looked down towards the rocks . . . and hesitated. There was a big difference between ordering Icarus to jump off the cliff and doing it himself. What if the wings didn't work? After all he was heavier than his son and anyway . . .

"Oi, Dedalus, where do you think you're goin'?"

"Yeah, goin'?"

Looking down, Icarus saw two men with his father. They were wearing the uniform of King Minos's guard. Both held drawn bows, with the arrows pointing straight at Dedalus. Fear surged through Icarus. Although his father spent every waking hour inventing new ways of putting him in danger, he didn't want to see Dedalus made into a pincushion.

On the cliff top, the soldiers gloated. "You're dead, Dedalus."

"Yeah, Dead-alas. Hur hur."

Knees knocking and teeth chattering, the old inventor stared death in the face. There was no escape. Even if he tried to fly away, the archers could hardly miss.

But as Dedalus gave himself up for lost, a shadow passed over him. He looked up. Minos's men screamed and dropped their bows, flinging themselves to the ground as Icarus swooped towards them. "Jump, Father!"

Dedalus jumped.

The shocked henchmen crawled to the cliff's edge and peered over to watch the crazed inventor plummet to his doom. Then they gasped in amazement as Dedalus swooped up and flew away from the rocks, the waves, his island prison and King Minos.

"See my boy! What a genius I am!" As they flew further from Crete, Icarus could hear Dedalus crowing triumphantly behind him. Now that the danger was past, the old man was full of himself.

"And when we reach the mainland, I can continue with my experiments. There are many more things for me to invent and for you to try out! I have so many ideas: ships that can sail under water, chariots that move without horses, shoes with wheels on. I can see them now!" He chuckled. "And you, Icarus, will have the honour of testing them out. You are going to have a great deal of fun!"

More like a great deal of bruises and broken bones, thought Icarus. They were flying over a smooth sea studded with small islands. Crete lay far behind them. It was time to put Perce's plan into action.

Icarus began to climb higher into the sky; further away from Dedalus and nearer to the sun.

"What are you doing, you fool?" A note of panic crept into Dedalus's voice. "You're going too high! The wax on your wings will melt! "

That's what I want you to think, grinned Icarus. He flew higher, straight towards the sun. Despite this, the air around him was growing colder, just as Perce had told him it would.

Dedalus squinted upwards. "Don't go near the sun, son!"

Icarus ignored his father and flew still higher.

Dedalus stared frantically into the blinding glare. "Where are you, boy? I can't see you!"

Good, thought Icarus. Then it's time.

He unstrapped his wings and flung them away. As he dropped from the sky, Icarus groped for the parachute's ripcord and hoped that Perce was right – that it would save him from falling to his death *and* from his father.

"Icarus? Where are you in Zeus' name?"

Dedalus saw the gleam of something white, far ahead. It spun crazily downwards through the sky and hit the sea with a splash. Horrified, Dedalus swooped downwards. The wreckage of Icarus's wings lay floating on the ocean.

"Icarus?" Dedalus circled mournfully around the wood and the feathers bobbing on the waves. "Achoo! Oh no! Icarus!"

He climbed away from the debris with a curse. "You stupid boy! I told you not to fly too close to the sun. Who am I going to get to carry out my experiments, now?"

The crazed inventor flew onwards, so busy moaning about his son's thoughtlessness that he never bothered to look up. If he had done so, he would have seen Icarus floating gently away under the canopy of his parachute.

Icarus landed in the water, released the parachute and kicked himself free. His father would be far away by now. Perce's plan had worked.

He peered into the distance and saw a small island. He would swim there and find work; perhaps become a shepherd, or keep goats. He liked animals. They didn't try to make him jump off cliffs.

Icarus would have liked to have stayed with the strangers in the future, who had been his friends for a short while. But their world wasn't his. This was where he belonged.

He began to swim towards the island and his new life.

Chapter Twelve

FLOATING ON AIR

"Do you reckon Liquorice survived?" asked Well'ard.

"I don't know. That's why we're here," answered Perce as she headed towards the reference books in the school library. She had insisted on meeting Well'ard, Eddie and Andy after school the next day.

"We could have done this at break," grumbled Well'ard.

"I was in detention at break, remember?"

"Why are you bothered about this Icarus anyway?" Andy was still in a bad mood after his high diving adventures. "I'm back safe and sound; isn't that the important thing?"

Perce just stared at him.

"She's bothered about him cos she fancied him," jeered Well'ard.

"Did you?" Andy gazed at her with narrowed eyes.

"No," said Perce, perhaps a little too quickly.

"What was he like?"

"Not like you at all," piped up Eddie.

"That's right," agreed Perce.

Andy beamed. Perce continued, "Not like you at all. He was intelligent, fun to be with, brave and . . ."

"You *did* fancy him." Andy was shocked.

"Just kidding. Anyway, he wasn't from this world and you can't fancy a myth can you?"

"S'pose not,' grunted Andy.

Perce took the Book of Myths off the shelf and turned to the Legend of Icarus.

"What's it say?" enquired Eddie.

"Hang on a sec." Perce began to read. "Icarus was a . . . blah, blah . . . His dad was Dedalus . . . blah, blah . . . He made some wings . . . blah, blah . . . He flew too close to the sun . . . blah, blah . . . The wax melted and he crashed into the sea and drowned."

"What a div!" exclaimed Well'ard. "We told 'im that was goin' to happen and he still went and did it! What an absolute . . ."

"Just a minute!" Perce was smiling. "Listen to this bit at the end: 'But some say that Icarus did not drown, but that the gods sent a small white cloud down from Olympus to bear him away to safety.'"

Well'ard looked blank.

"The parachute," explained Perce. "That was the cloud! It didn't come from Olympus, the home of the gods, it came from the airfield. Icarus did survive!"

She was interrupted by Mr Latimer's voice outside the library door. "Mrs Jones! Have you seen Priscilla? I've just received a message from the attendant at the swimming pool. Apparently the pool was covered in feathers again last night! If I find she had anything to do with it . . ."

Perce led the others in a charge out of the back door of the library.

On the way to her house, Perce told Andy about her brilliant plan to get him back and save Icarus. She'd already told Andy all about this, but she thought he ought to hear it again anyway, just in case he'd forgotten how brilliant she'd been. Eddie and Well'ard wanted Perce to leave out the stuff about well'ard mallards, Alsatians and swans, but she didn't.

Turning into Perce's drive, they suddenly stopped dead. From the shouts and bangs that were coming from inside the house, there was obviously a major row brewing.

"Look what I've found in the dustbin! The cover from my best duvet!" Perce's mother sounded furious. "All the feathers are gone! What would your stupid daughter want with feathers?"

"She's your stupid daughter as well."

"She's in big trouble when she gets in, I can tell you."

Perce grimaced and hurried out of the drive.

"Er, I reckon we won't bother going in just now. Maybe a bit later when the wrinklies have cooled down, like in a million years. Let's go somewhere else."

"We can't go to my house," growled Well'ard. "For some reason, my dad's blaming me cos he's lost his fishing net."

Eddie looked quizzical. "But you are to blame. You nicked it and the Alsatian ate it."

"So? That's no reason to accuse me, just cos I did it."

There was silence for a couple of minutes as they all tried to work out Well'ard's illogical logic.

"Well, how about going swimming?" suggested Eddie.

"No way!" cried Andy.

"What about the park?" asked Perce sweetly. "Oh no, sorry boys, I forgot there's some big hard ducks there!"

Eddie and Well'ard glared at Perce.

"I know!" Perce snapped her fingers. "Follow me."

She led the way through the streets of the town, ignoring all the boys' questions. She eventually stopped outside the amusement arcade.

"Here we go." Perce bought a token from the desk and propelled Andy through the doorway of a large white machine. "Strap up," she told him.

"Why? What is this?" hissed Andy.

Perce grinned wickedly. "It's a Flight Simulator." Well'ard and Eddie burst out laughing.

Andy turned as white as a feather. "You must be joking."

"Don't get into a flap, you chicken. I dare you."

But Perce was talking to empty air. Andy, moving as if he had wings on his feet, flew out of the arcade, down the street and disappeared from sight.

About the authors

STEVE BARLOW was born in Crewe but now lives in Somerset with his wife and cats. After working as a puppeteer, refuse collector and laundry van driver, he became a teacher of the performing arts, before turning to full time writing.

STEVE SKIDMORE was born in Leicester. He trained as a teacher and met Steve Barlow at a school in Nottingham nearly twenty years ago. They began writing plays for their students and haven't looked back.

"THE 2 STEVES" are Britain's most popular writing double act for young people, specializing in comedy and adventure. They perform regularly in schools and libraries, delighting audiences of all ages.

To find out more about "THE 2 STEVES" visit their website *www.the2steves.net*

STONE ME!

by Steve Barlow & Steve Skidmore

Illustrated by Tony Ross

ISBN 1-903015-43-X £4.99

When a rather dramatic new supply teacher comes to the school called Ms Dusa and she wears a large turban over her hair, Perce and Andy get suspicious. After several children get turned to stone the duo realize they are right, this is indeed Medusa come into the 21st Century. As none of the grown ups seem to rumble as to what is happening, Perce and Andy decide that action needs to be taken and they are the ones to take it!

A hilarious take on the ancient Greek myth that is both entertaining and informative.

MIND THE DOOR!

by Steve Barlow & Steve Skidmore

Illustrated by Tony Ross

ISBN 1-903015-49-9 £4.99

The new school caretaker has Perce worried. Not just because he's got a body like King Kong's brother. Nor because he wears a trendy nose-ring. It's just that he seems – well, a bit of a bully. Andy couldn't care less. He thinks Mr O'Taur is the best thing since microwave popcorn. But then kids start to go missing from Mr O'Taur's gym club. And when the terrible secret of the Labyrinth is revealed, Perce, Andy, Well'ard and Eddie Johnson realize that they have the bull by the horns and their lives are hanging by a thread . . . (Well, okay, a loo roll. . .).

A madcap retelling of the Minotaur Myth by 'The 2 Steves.'